Acting Edition

August Wilson's

How I Learned What I Learned

(And How What I Learned Has Led Me to Places I've Wanted to Go. That I Have Sometimes Gone Unwillingly is the Crucible in Which Many a Work of Art Has Been Fired.)

Co-conceived by Todd Kreidler

This work is published by Samuel French, an imprint of Concord Theatricals Corp.

No one shall make any changes in this title(s) for the purpose of production. No part of this book may be reproduced, stored in a retrieval system, scanned, uploaded, or transmitted in any form, by any means, now known or yet to be invented, including mechanical, electronic, digital, photocopying, recording, videotaping, or otherwise, without the prior written permission of the publisher. No one shall share this title(s), or any part of this title(s), through any social media or file hosting websites.

For all inquiries regarding motion picture, television, online/digital and other media rights, please contact Concord Theatricals Corp.

MUSIC AND THIRD-PARTY MATERIALS USE NOTE

Licensees are solely responsible for obtaining formal written permission from copyright owners to use copyrighted music and/or other copyrighted third-party materials (e.g. artworks, logos) in the performance of this play and are strongly cautioned to do so. If no such permission is obtained by the licensee, then the licensee must use only original music and materials that the licensee owns and controls. Licensees are solely responsible and liable for clearances of all third-party copyrighted materials, including without limitation music, and shall indemnify the copyright owners of the play(s) and their licensing agent, Concord Theatricals Corp., against any costs, expenses, losses and liabilities arising from the use of such copyrighted third-party materials by licensees. For music, please contact the appropriate music licensing authority in your territory for the rights to any incidental music.

IMPORTANT BILLING AND CREDIT REQUIREMENTS

If you have obtained performance rights to this title, please refer to your licensing agreement for important billing and credit requirements.

HOW I LEARNED WHAT I LEARNED had its world premiere presented by Seattle Repertory Theatre (Sharon Ott, Artistic Director; Benjamin Moore, Managing Director) on May 22, 2003, performed by August Wilson. The director was Todd Kreidler, the lighting designer was L. B. Morse, and the production stage manager was Michael Paul.

The New York premiere was originally produced by Signature Theatre, New York City (James Houghton, Founding Artistic Director; Erika Mallin, Executive Director) on November 24, 2013. The director was Todd Kreidler in collaboration with and featuring Ruben Santiago-Hudson, the creative consultant and costume designer was Constanza Romero, the scenic & projection designer was David Gallo, the lighting designer was Thom Weaver, the sound designer was Dan Moses Schreier, and the production stage manager was Winnie Y. Lok.

The Atlanta premiere was produced by True Colors Theatre Company (Kenny Leon, Founder & Artistic Director; Jennifer Dwyer McEwen, Executive Director) on October 7, 2014 and performed by Eugene Lee. The director was Todd Kreidler, the creative consultant and costume designer was Constanza Romero, the scenic & projection designer was David Gallo, the lighting designer was Thom Weaver, the sound designer was Dan Moses Schreier, and the production stage manager was Lisa L. Watson.

The Pittsburgh premiere was produced by Pittsburgh Public Theater (Ted Pappas, Producing Artistic Director) on March 5, 2015 and performed by Eugene Lee. The director was Todd Kreidler, the creative consultant and costume designer was Constanza Romero, the scenic & projection designer was David Gallo, the lighting designer was Thom Weaver, the sound designer was Dan Moses Schreier, and the production stage manager was Fred Noel.

The Boston premiere was produced by The Huntington Theatre Company (Peter DuBois, Artistic Director; Michael Maso, Managing Director) on March 5, 2016 and performed by Eugene Lee. The director was Todd Kreidler, the creative consultant and costume designer was Constanza Romero, the scenic & projection designer was David Gallo, the lighting designer was Thom Weaver, the sound designer was Dan Moses Schreier, the production stage manager was Carola Morrone LaCoste, and the stage manager was Jeremiah Mullane.

HOW I LEARNED WHAT I LEARNED was subsequently produced by Round House Theatre (Ryan Rilette, Artistic Director; Ed Zakreski, Managing Director) on June 7, 2017 and performed by Eugene Lee. The director was Todd Kreidler, the creative consultant and costume designer was Constanza Romero, the scenic & projection designer was David Gallo, the lighting designer was Thom Weaver, the sound designer was Dan Moses Schreier, and the production stage manager was Che Wernsman.

CHARACTERS

ACTOR

SETTING

The crucible in which many a work of art has been fired.

(The setting is the crucible in which many a work of art has been fired. There is a stool, a coat rack, and atop a desk, Webster's Third New International Dictionary.)

(An idyllic song celebrating America booms in preshow.*)

(House lights fade out.)

("Run, Old Jeremiah" plays as lights reveal an ACTOR sitting on a stool. He wears a sport coat and cap. The lighting tight, formal, the feel of a lecture.)

(Projected letters type out...)

MY ANCESTORS

My ancestors have been in America since the early seventeenth century. And for the first two hundred and forty-four years we never had a problem finding a job. But since 1863 it's been hell. It's been hell because the ideas and attitudes that America had toward slaves followed them out of slavery and became entrenched in the nation's psyche. Ideas that said that Blacks were sub-human, that they were lacking in moral personality, that they were unbaptizeable, that they were lazy, shiftless, watermelon-eating, chicken-stealing, oversexed, loud, menacing appendages to the polite, civilized society that the Europeans had wrestled from, what the Honorable Elijah Muhammad called "the wilderness of North America." This is, after the polite, civilized Europeans had killed all the Indians.

In early 1900s we cast down our buckets where we were and they came up empty. And filled with the blood and bile of countless murders and unwanted assaults against our

---

*Licensees should use a song in the public domain or create an original composition.

person. So, we brought our buckets North searching for jobs and opportunity to live life with dignity and whatever eloquence the heart could call upon.

My mother came from Spear, North Carolina in 1937 and settled in a neighborhood (here) in Pittsburgh called the Hill District. In the Hill District in 1937 was an amalgam of the unwanted – Blacks, Syrians, Jews, Italians, Irish, with each ethnic group seeking to cast off the vestiges of the old country, changing names, changing manners and given a myriad of unlimited opportunities changing economic circumstance and moving out, up, in, bludgeoning the malleable parts of themselves. Melting into the pot. Becoming and defining what it means to be an American.

(A happy instrumental ditty plays as lights brighten.*)

(The ACTOR crosses to the coat rack, removes his hat and sport coat, revealing the back of his T-shirt...)

I AM AN

ACCIDENT

THIS DID NOT

TURN OUT RIGHT

(He turns to reveal the front of his T-shirt...)

I AM

SUPPOSED

TO BE

WHITE

Like my T-shirt? I got this on Ebay. Got it from a man named Clarence Thomas. I saw this and said, "Oh, I've got to get this for my man, Justin Bieber."

I met Fred Rogers once in Pittsburgh at WQED television station. As I was leaving, Fred Rogers shook my hand and said, "You're always welcome in this neighborhood." You see, Fred Rogers will never know what that meant

---

*Licensees should use a song in the public domain or create an original composition.

to me. See, because they weren't saying that in 1957 when we moved into Hazelwood on Flowers Avenue when they threw bricks into the window with a note tied around it that said, "Stay out niggers." And they weren't saying that in 1955 when Monsignor Connare preached his now famous sermon, informing the parishioners that the Catholic Church in the Hill District was now going to accept Negroes as parishioners and that those that didn't like it should leave the church. And the next Sunday, there weren't nobody in church, except for three, little, old ladies over here. See, we all know them three, little, old ladies. They everywhere. And if the country was made up of them three, little, old ladies we'd be alright. See, because they weren't concerned about sitting next to Negroes at church. As long as they get their Social Security check and the supermarket don't run out of cat food then they doing alright. But, the Vatican was concerned about it. The Vatican didn't even know that St. Richards Church existed, until the parishioners left. See, because the contributions went down from $2,000 a week to $137, then that got the attention of the Catholic Church. Monsignor Connare got fired. That's when I knew that the Catholic Church was immoral. Because if they had any morality he would've got a promotion.

Who were these people who left the church? That threw bricks through the window at 85 Flowers Avenue with a note tied around it saying, "Stay out nigger"? They were good, honest Americans, not unlike yourselves. Good, honest Americans concerned about paying their mortgage, concerned about the future of their kids, concerned about consolidating and protecting the position that they had earned in American society over the past forty years, starting in 1915 when they came over with the wave of European immigrants. Good, honest Americans who were victims of a linguistic environment that said, *(At dictionary.)* according to *Webster's Third New International Dictionary* that Blacks were "outrageously wicked, dishonorable, connected with the devil, menacing, sullen, hostile, unqualified, violators of public regulations and affected by an undesirable condition." Hell, I would've left the church too. Who wants to go to church with some outrageously wicked people, who are connected to the devil and who are sullen, hostile and menacing and chicken thieves to boot? Especially, if you were, *(At dictionary.)* according to *Webster's Third New International Dictionary*, and you were white, that you were "outstandingly righteous, free from blemish, moral stain or impurity. Innocent, not marked by malignant influence. Notably auspicious, fortunate, decent, sterling."

Every child acquires the language, eating habits, gestures, notions of common sense, the attitudes towards sex, the concepts of beauty and justice and the responses to pleasure and pain from the people who raise them. These ideas and attitudes have been passed down from generation to generation and we have inherited them. They are an inheritance unworthy of our grandchildren, because it puts an encumbrance on their lives. Yet, these attitudes are still alive today.

I was just at a fundraising event for the Huntington Theatre when a man walked up to me and he shook my hand and he said, "Mr. Wilson, you know I don't see color." And, I heard this a thousand times and I was tired of hearing it. So, I said, "Did you tell that gentleman over here that?" And I pointed to a white man. He looked at me puzzled. And I said, "Did you tell that gentleman over there that?" And I pointed to another white man. And I said, "Why, since you don't see color, why of all the people in the room did you walk up to me and say that?" And he looked at me and said, "You're being sensitive." Then he turned and walked off.

What he was really saying was that he could accept the fact of my humanity as long as he could ignore my color. That he was willing to accept me as long as I was wearing this T-shirt, that says that "I'm Supposed to be White," and that I am Black by the accident of my birth.

An accident is where something goes wrong. Like you might have a friend of yours who's in an automobile accident and you see him and he's lost his arm. You see him and say, "Hey, Joe, man gee I'm sorry that happened."

See, people will walk up to you and when you Black and look at you and say, "You got fucked up man. I'm sorry that happened, because you otherwise a nice guy."

We are not Black by the accident of our births. Our births are moments of profound creativity engineered by our genetic muscle as it aspires toward perfection.

> *("Run, Old Jeremiah" begins to play as* **ACTOR** *removes T-shirt.)*

This music that you are hearing is not recorded in Africa, it was recorded in Louisiana in 1934. We are an African people and we have an honorable history in the world of men.

> *(An African dance as music grows.)*

> *(Typing...)*

HILL DISTRICT

The bridge where I sit shakes
As the busses roll over it.
Around me, the hills, frantic
With houses, the hills
Rising above the river,
Hills nippled with houses.
As though I returned, as easily,
These things come back.
Old things without a stitch
In time, but somewhere
Echoed on the nerve.

> *(Additional typing...)*

1965

The Hill District in 1965 was a community of 55,000 people. That's 54,997 Blacks and them three little old ladies. Using the statistics by which you measure a peoples' health, per capita income, infant mortality rate, life expectancy – the Hill District in 1965 was a third-world country. And yet, it's only a four-minute walk to downtown Pittsburgh with its cornucopia of riches. Despite its poverty the Hill District is a vibrant, if not thriving community. There are nine drugstores, all of which are within a five-minute walk of each other. You've got Taxey Drugs, Jay's Drugs, Hill Pharmacy, Mid-Center Drug, Chauncy Drug, Pure Drug. Nine drugstores, three wallpaper and paint stores, two lumberyards, a live fish market, four funeral homes, eighteen barbershops, thirteen beauty salons and one hundred and forty-seven bars. That's one on each corner and four in between. Eighty-two churches and one supermarket, the Mainway Supermarket. Mainway Supermarket was the first business to burn during the riots following Martin Luther King's assassination in 1968. It was the first place to burn because the owners overcharged us and they were disrespectful and the people hated shopping there.

Oh, I may as well tell you all this now, because I want you to know, I want everybody to know. I did not burn down the Mainway Supermarket, during the riots in 1968. There's some people who think I did. But, I just want you all to know, I did not. But it is true that I had my picture taken standing triumphantly in the smoldering ruins, but I did not burn down the Mainway. I was just a man who recognized a good photo opportunity when he saw one.

There are four streets, all running parallel to one another. Bedford Avenue, where I was born and raised at 1727 Bedford Avenue, and where my sister lived at 1615 Bedford Avenue, and where my mother lived until she died in 1983, at 1621 Bedford Avenue. Four streets – Bedford Avenue, Webster, Wiley and Center Avenue, what we called "The Set."

   (Typing…)

THE SET

The main drag, the Set, the stage where life is played out. At any given moment down on the Set, you are liable to look up and see two hundred to three hundred people standing on the corner. What they doing? They looking for opportunity. But the opportunities available to them are not the same opportunities available to say someone who lives in Squirrel Hill. The opportunity to get a job selling neckties in a department store and work your way up to become manager of the Men's Clothing Department. Opportunity to go to college for social or personal advancement. Opportunity to take over your father's business. No. The opportunities on Center Avenue in 1965 was the opportunity to die an early death. Opportunity to buy some dope. Opportunity to steal something. And if you're lucky, an opportunity to maybe find a girlfriend.

At the age of fifteen, I dropped out of school, but I didn't drop out of life. I went to the library. At the age of twenty, I left the library and I left my mother's house and I went down on the Set, the main drag, Pittsburgh. And here I fell into the clutches of a group of poets and painters at the Hill Arts Society. Chawley Williams, Barbara Peterson, Cy Morocco, Dingbat, Nick Flourney, Levy Shaud, Rob Penny, Gerry Rhodes. People who became my life-long friends and, ultimately, sanctioned my life and provided it with its meaning.

Chawley Williams was ten years older than me. Chawley was a poet. Chawley took me under his wing. One day Chawley said, "August, when you go to jail, man, call Al Liechtenstein, he's the best lawyer in Pittsburgh." You notice he didn't say, "*If* you go to jail." He said, "*When* you go to jail." Because as a twenty-year-old Black man in the Hill District in Pittsburgh in 1965 you going to jail.

After leaving your mother's house, the first thing you discover is that you gotta pay the rent. See, I found me a place at 85 Crawford Street. It was a two-room, basement apartment down under this porch. An apartment befitting a young twenty-year-old poet. And the rent was $25 every two weeks. And you have no idea how much money that was.

In 1965 you could walk into any bar in Pittsburgh and get a bottle of beer for a quarter. Pack of cigarettes was thirty-one cents. Three pounds of ground meat was a dollar. Ten pounds of potatoes was thirty-nine cents. A pound of margarine twenty-five cents. Twenty-five dollars in 1965 was a lot of money. And I was a poet at the time and I can remember that one day I typed up my best poem. It was an eighteen-line poem and I typed it up and I sent it to *Harper's Magazine.* I sent it to *Harper's* because they paid a dollar a line. And, the other magazines paid twenty-five cents, thirty cents a line. And as I was putting the poem in the envelope an idea occurred to me that would've made my seventh-grade math teacher, Sister Mary Eldephonse, proud of me. You see I retyped that poem and I broke it up into thirty-six lines, just in case. Three days later it was back in my mailbox. And I go oh, I see, this is serious. August, you're going to have to learn to write a poem. So, I set myself on this concerted effort to learn how to write poetry.

(Typing...)

BARBARA PETERSON

My next door neighbor at 85 Crawford Street was Barbara Peterson. Barbara was a painter. Barbara wanted to go to Carnegie Mellon University. It was called Carnegie Tech at the time. But, Barbara couldn't get in. Why? You know. She was outrageously wicked. Violator of public regulations. Sullen, hostile, menacing and affected by an undesirable condition. See, but Barbara was a smart woman. Barbara got in the classroom. Barbara took a job modeling in the classroom. She listened to the instructor and she did the work and she showed it to him. And because he was a man who wasn't a victim of the linguistic environment in America he got her a scholarship. And when she died an untimely death in 1982 at the age of forty-two, Barbara was in charge of art at the Pittsburgh Public School System. And I told myself, that was my first real lesson in life. I said, "August, there's a way under, around or through any door." I said, "Okay, yeah, I got that." But what I ain't got is this twenty-five dollars.

(Typing...)

MAN WANTED:
STOCKROOM, TOY STORE

Man wanted: Stockroom, toy store. Yeah, that's me. I went down and applied for the job. I got hired. The man said come to work at nine o'clock tomorrow. I was there at ten minutes to nine. See, because my mother had a thing about punctuality. And my mother said, "You gotta be somewhere at nine o'clock, why not be there at ten minutes to, that way you always be on time." So, I was there. And I showed up and he's showing me around the stockroom and said this is where we keep this kind of toys, this is where we keep these kind of toys, and this is where we keep these kind of toys. And he said, "Your job is to get these toys and put this over…" And I said, "Yeah, yeah. Okay, I got that." Then he looked at me and he said, "Now, if I catch you stealing anything, I'm gonna shoot you." A toy. I'm gonna steal a goddamn toy? You see, because he ain't got nothing to steal. He trying to get. If he wasn't in with the Wall Street crowd of his day, he ain't got nothing. He in debt. I don't owe nobody nothing. He drowning. I'm treading water, but he going under. You see, because they fixing to foreclose on his store, his house and his car. He got more reason to steal than anybody. "If I catch you stealing anything, I'm gonna shoot you." I wanted to tell him to "kiss my ass." But, being my mother's son, I politely told him, "I quit. Motherfucker."

(*Typing…*)

WANTED: MAN TO CUT GRASS

Wanted: Man to cut grass. That's me.

I had a grass-cutting business when I was fourteen. I had twelve customers and I was good at it. Some of the guys in the neighborhood tried to take my job, but they go "No, no we got somebody to cut our lawn." A man named Pat Zatola. Italian, Catholic – Pat hired me. And he would pick me up at 6:30 in the morning, in downtown Pittsburgh and we'd drive twenty miles out to Mount Lebanon, to Greentree, to Castle Shannon and cut people's lawns until 10:30 at night. And Pat would say, "Go cut that lawn." And I'd go cut that lawn. Pat would say, "Go and cut that lawn." And I'd go cut that lawn. "Go and cut that lawn." And I'd go and cut that lawn, until one day Pat said, "Go and cut that lawn." And I was cutting the lawn and a woman come out of the house and she was yelling at Pat. And she was saying something that I couldn't hear, so I cut off the lawnmower so I could hear what she was saying. And she was saying, "Get him off my lawn. Get him off my lawn." And then Pat come over to me and said, "Go cut the next lawn." And I said, "You told me to cut this lawn." He said, "Well, go cut the next lawn." I said, "Yeah, I will *after* I cut this lawn." And Pat said, "Go and cut the next lawn." And I said, "I quit."

Okay, now I'm mad. Disappointed and I still ain't got no job and I'm twenty miles outside of Pittsburgh. More importantly, I was a witness to Pat Zatola's moral failure, which I watched him sell to that woman for five dollars. You see, he's so busy patting himself on the back for hiring me, a Black man, that he can't see where the real moral challenge is. Because he should've told her, "Nah, he works for me. And if you don't want him to cut your lawn, then I don't want your business." But that's not what he told her. He took the five dollars.

See, that reminds me of Judas. See, because Judas betrayed Jesus Christ for a measly thirty pieces of silver, it wasn't even gold. For five dollars. Now, I could've went and cut the next lawn and kept my job.

I could've ignored the fact that the man at the toy store called me a thief before I started. See, but I'm my mother's son. I had learned from my mother that something is not always better than nothing.

(Typing…)

SOMETHING IS NOT ALWAYS BETTER
THAN NOTHING

See, and I learned this because my mother won a radio contest one time. It was a radio contest, and it was sponsored by the radio station and you named the product. They gave you the slogan and if you could name the product then you were the winner of a brand new Speed Queen washing machine. And see, my mother, at the time, had four kids and she was scrubbing the clothes on a washboard. And the question was, "When it rains, it pours." What's the product? Morton salt. See, my mother knew that. And my mother was the first one to call up the radio station. They announced her name over the radio, said, "Daisy Wilson. The winner of a brand new Speed Queen washing machine." And then they found out that my mother was Black. And they wanted to give her a certificate to go to the Salvation Army and get a used washing machine. And my mother said, "No." And I can remember her friend, Julie Burley, saying to her, "Daisy, what difference it make. You got all those kids. Go get, take the washing machine. It'd make your work so much easier." And my mother looked at her and she said, "Something is not always better than nothing."

And then my mother went and took this mayonnaise jar and she reached in her apron pocket and took out a dime and she dropped it in the mayonnaise jar. And that dime became the first dime toward the eighty-nine dollars that a brand new Speed Queen washing machine cost. You see and she wasn't going to have no other kind. And when she dropped that dime in there I said, "Oh man, I ain't gonna get no nickels for a long time." But being my mother's son, I went out and found two pop bottles and cashed them in for two cents apiece. And I brought her the four cents and I said, "Ma, this is for the washing machine." I want to tell you it was a great day, about a year and a half later, when that brand new Speed Queen washing machine came into the house. I'm not going to tell you all how I broke it.

(Typing...)

WANTED:
MAN TO WASH DISHES

Wanted: Man to wash dishes? ...I don't know, I ain't never washed dishes before.

See, I grew up in a house with three older sisters, but I'm game. You know? I got hired. Klein's Restaurant on Fourth Avenue in downtown Pittsburgh. And a man named Ned ran the kitchen. And see, we all know Ned. Ned is the man who married the boss' daughter. See, otherwise the best Ned could do is sell newspapers on the corner. But see, right now he a big man in the kitchen. And one day, as

I was putting the dishes through, they had a metal plate on the dishwasher that said to keep the temperature at 120 degrees. You see that's the degrees in which water kills germs. And I said, "That's science." And I was putting the soap in and I read the ingredients of the soap and I said, "That's chemistry." And I looked at the plate and I said, "That's ceramics." And so, following this trail I began to go to the library and that led me to Claude Levi Strauss' *The Origins of Table Manners*. That led me to reading about culinary arts. And that led me to reading about agricultural techniques, which led to the cattle ranchers and the sheep ranchers in the Old West, which led to the settling of the West, which led to Custer, which led to Cochise, which led to the Mexicans, which led to the Catholics, which led to Catholicism, which led to the Pope, which led to Pope Pius the Twelfth silenced on the Holocaust and World War II, which led to Pope John the Twenty-Third, which led to Matthew, Mark, John, Luke, Judas, the betrayal. Famous betrayals in history. Which led to beds, brass beds, canopy beds and I'm following this line, this trail of things and one day I'm coming through the kitchen and I had my books under my arm. And Ned said to me, "What are the books for?" And I looked at him like he was crazy. I said, "They're to read." See, I noticed after that that Ned began to watch me and look at me strange. And one day I came back from lunch and I was coming through the dining room and Ned was standing in the middle of the dining room and he looked at me and he looked at his watch and he said, "You're twenty seconds late coming back from lunch." And I said, "Well, it took me twenty seconds to come through the dining room. I tell you what. Since you counting seconds. It's going to take me fifty-four seconds to go down to there and get my books and the rest of my things and have my money ready for me when I come up. 'Cause I quit." And I went down and got my books and I got my things and I come up and I asked for my money. Ned told me to "come back Tuesday." And I said, "No, you don't understand. I ain't quitting on Tuesday, I quit now. And I want my money. I don't want your money. I want *my* money. And if you don't give it to me, you gonna have to kill me." And see, I meant it because I was willing and ready to die. He must of understood that because he gave me my money.

(*Typing…*)

JAIL

J-A-I-L. I wasn't out of my mother's house but four months and I look up and find myself in jail. And it wasn't over no civil rights march either. It was over that twenty-five dollars. See, when you can't pay the rent you gotta go talk to your landlord. See, Mr. Jackson, he don't own the place. He collecting money for the white man who owns the place and he get his rent for free, as long as he can collect the money. He got a good thing going and here you come to fuck it up. "Uh, Mr. Jackson sir, I can't pay you today." Say, "I'll pay you on Tuesday." And Tuesday come and say, "Mr. Jackson, things didn't work out like I thought, I can't pay you 'til Friday." And then Friday it's, "Mr. Jackson, I can't pay you 'til Monday." And see, all the time you getting further and further behind. So, one day being a young man looking for female companionship, I went out and met this woman. And I said to her, I said, "Baby, why don't you come on down to the house and let me show you my record collection." And so, she said, "Okay." And we go down to the house and we get there and there's a padlock on the door. See, because I owe Mr. Jackson about fifty dollars in back rent. So, I say, "Come on baby, there's a phone booth on the corner here. I gotta go make a phone call." See, because I knew this lawyer. His name was Steve Bartoromo. I knew Steve because my father had just died and Steve Bartoromo was handling his estate. And Steve's mother, Mary Bartoromo lived three doors down from my mother. And my mother takes her shopping. And Mary Bartoromo likes to brag on her son. So, I knew that he was number one in his class in law school. So, if anybody know about this, Steve Bartoromo do. So, I call him up and say, "Steve man, this is August. No, no I ain't calling about that. Say listen, Steve can a landlord put a lock on your door if you owe him some back rent?" He go, "No, he's not allowed to do that. You know, he's got to give you a thirty-day notice." So, I say, "Mean, I could bust the lock off and ain't nothing gonna happen to me?" He go, "Yeah, you could bust it off. He's not allowed to do that. He's gotta give you a thirty-day notice." "Yeah, thanks Steve. Come on, baby." Then I went on down and took a brick and busted off the lock and went on in.

To my surprise, when I wake up in the morning there were two policemen standing over me. Saying, "Come on buddy, let's go." I said, "Come on what? I ain't done nothing. My lawyer told me." [The policemen say] "Come on buddy, let's go." But they were nice. They went in the room, while the woman got dressed. And I asked them not to handcuff me and they said, "Okay." See, because somehow I feel if they put them handcuffs on me that that would mark me for life. See, so they agreed not to handcuff me. But, I do want you to know that there's a whole bunch of niggers that they do handcuff.

So, they take me down to jail. See and I'm mad, because I ain't done nothing. Come to find out, ain't nobody down here done nothing. So I call up Steve and I explain the situation to him. Steve say, "I'll be right down." Well, morning passed into afternoon and Steve ain't come. And afternoon pass into evening. And I find out that seven o'clock is the time that they lock you up. See, up until that time you free to, you know, roam around, play cards and dominoes with the inmates and what not. But, seven o'clock they lock you up in your individual cell. And you have to be quiet from then on. And like sure enough there are bars in front of you and the door is locked and you can't get out. I want you to understand, you cannot get out. But, like, I ain't in jail 'cause I ain't done nothing, right? And then I hear an inmate singing…

> (An offstage voice sings "Nobody Knows The Trouble I've Seen.")

"I'm in jail, man. I'm in jail." I cried like a baby. It's the most humbling experience. But see, he had a good voice and the guards let him sing to eight o'clock. Then I found out he took requests. 'Cause after he finished singing that song a guy goes, "After You've Gone. After You've Gone." And I thought that he was asking the guy who was singing the song when he got out. But, that was his song request. You know, for a song called "After You've Gone." So, the guy started singing, "After you've gone and left me cryin' / After you've gone there's no denyin' / You feel blue, you feel sad / You miss the greatest love you ever had…" I didn't even have a girlfriend and I started crying. And I found out later that that's a famous composition. Bessie Smith made that song famous, man. I was in jail the first time I heard that. And I always wondered if Bessie Smith may've been in jail the first time she heard it too. Anyway, it took them three days to get it all straightened out. Three days! And finally, they called me and they said, "Okay, you can go." And they let me out. Then one of the guards said, "What's with him?" [The other guard said] "Oh, he was acting under advice of counsel." See, and I found out what had happened was a landlord is allowed to padlock the door if it's a furnished apartment. He's not allowed to padlock an unfurnished apartment. And leaving out that little, significant fact cost me three days of my life. You see, because if Steve had told me, "No, man you can't bust that lock off the door." Then I wouldn't have busted it off. Because the reason I asked him is because I don't want to go to jail. And if he had said, "No, you can't do that." Then I would've said to her, "Let's go look at your record collection." So, now I'm on the four-minute walk to 85 Crawford Street and I don't know what made me think I'm gonna go back and live in my apartment. You see, but Mr. Jackson done rented that out in them three days to somebody else. And more important than that, he got all my clothes and little bit of stuff and my poems. And say, he ain't going to give them to me until I pay the back rent. You see, now, I'm ready to go to jail, for something. And I told him. Well, I ain't going to tell you what I told him. But, it was something like if he didn't give me my things then I was going to cut him up in little pieces and drag his bones out to the edge of the city and boil them in pig's blood. See and he must've believed me because he gave me back my poems.

(The **ACTOR** *discovers a poem buried in the dirt...)*

The garden
Is burning. The cauldron boiling –
Come to add to the brute
Spectacle of things on the heart.
Things hidden over. Covered
with the visage of the city:
Rivers, hills with houses,
Bridges stretched from point
To point. Old bridges that
Creak and shake in the sun.

So, now I'm standing here with my poetry in the middle of Crawford Street. So, what to do? "Ma?" Yeah, I went back up to my mother's house.

(Typing...)

THE HILL ARTS SOCIETY

The Hill Arts Society. There's a restaurant called Pope's, which is right next door to The Hill Arts Society. I don't know what the circumstances or the situation was, but The Hill Arts Society had a boycott going at Pope's. Wasn't nobody patronizing Pope's. And I joined the boycott. Matter of fact, I would stand there and if I saw somebody going into Pope's. I'd tell them, "No, we ain't going in there. It's a boycott."

One day I was walking by Pope's and I see that Pope's got a new waitress. Man, I broke the boycott. I walked in and I said, "Hi." And she said, "Hi." And I found out her name was Willa Mae Montay. Otherwise known as Snookie...

(Typing...)

SNOOKIE

...And I found out that she was married to a man named Billy. And Billy was a janitor in the Pittsburgh Public

Schools, but her and Billy were separated and Billy had moved out the house about two months before.

So, I got to talking with her and she handed me something and she said, "Here, walk around the corner and smoke this." And I looked at it and it was a reefer, you know like marijuana. And in 1965 this was illegal. Well, it's still illegal today, mostly. And I had never seen any reefer before. But I walked outside and walked around the corner and I lit it. You know? Yeah. I walked around the corner and smoked it.

I don't know what it was, the reefer must've made my game real smooth. You see, because she gave me her tips, which was three dollars. She gave me the three dollars and there was a guy that was courting her that worked at a bakery nearby and he brought her a cake. And, she gave me the cake too. And I rode with her in a jitney and waited, because it was a little cool out. And I waited while she threw one of her husband's coats out the window and then I rode back with the jitney driver. It was like, all of sudden life got good. I got her tips, a cake, I got me a woman and I got me a new coat. I couldn't wait until the sun come up the next day. I told Snookie, "Come on, let's go on a date." I got three dollars.

So, we went down to the Oyster House, downtown Pittsburgh. Fish sandwich costs thirty-five cents.

Now, see at that time, I was reading these short stories by Guy de Maupassant and they were these short stories about these Prussian officers who were always defending the honor of their women and always challenging other men to duels, and things like that there. And you know I liked that, I found that stuff exciting.

So, we go on down there and we having a nice time and Snookie has to go to the bathroom. So, she asked the bartender where the bathroom was. And he said, "Upstairs." And I said, "Excuse me man, this a lady, man. And it's 'Upstairs, ma'am.' Show some respect... This a woman, man. Matter a fact, this my woman. You're supposed to show some respect. You're supposed to say, 'The bathroom's upstairs, ma'am.'" And he said, "Go on, buddy." And I said, "Well you know, we could settle this with a duel." And see, that's when I found out that he wasn't reading the same books that I was. 'Cause he reached under the counter and pulled out a double-barrel shotgun and pointed it at me and told me to leave. And when he pulled out the double-barrel shotgun, I started laughing. Because all I could think of was Elmer Fudd and Bugs Bunny. And I'm looking at this shotgun and saying, "Wow, that's real, they actually do make them. I thought that was just in cartoons." See now, I don't know if you've ever had a double-barrel shotgun pointed at you before, but, you see, the barrels, the size of the barrels are in proportion to your fear. See, and they look like hubcaps. But, I couldn't let him know that so I started laughing. And I go, "Yeah, yeah. Okay, yeah, yeah. Come on baby. Yeah, okay yeah. Right." Then at the door, I announced in my best Douglas MacArthur voice, "I shall return." And we got the hell out of there. Then Snookie says, "What'd you do that for? I still got to pee."

Time go along, things got good between me and Snookie. And in January, she invited me to move in with her. And, I did. And I got this job working in the mailroom at Krogers. So, I got this job and see if you're a young, twenty-year-old poet and you get a job in the mailroom, that's good. You know, free supplies. I don't know why it is what makes you think if you had twelve pens you could write a better poem than if you had one pen. So, I had me some supplies.

So, Valentine's Day was coming up and Snookie said, "Why don't you meet me at the 88 Bar after work and we'll celebrate Valentine's Day." See, but unbeknownst to Snookie, I had some Valentine's Day plans of my own. See, I'm working. I'm making sixty-one dollars a week. And, I got some tickets for the Ella Fitzgerald concert that was going to be at the Civic Arena. And they were opening up the dome and it was going to be a Valentine's Day concert under the stars. So, I got dressed that morning to go to work and I put on my best clothes and I couldn't wait to get off work. And, finally five o'clock comes and I got off work and I jumped on that bus and bust into the 88 Bar and I see Snookie with her husband, Billy. Now, there's something inside me that just does not allow me to turn and walk out the door. So, I figure I'd go down this aisle and go to the bathroom and then walk out. So, it make it look like I just come in to go to the bathroom. So, I start down the aisle and then I hear her call me, "August, come here." So, I go around and sit down. "I want to introduce you to Billy. Billy, this is August. August, this is Billy."

"How you doing, man."

Then Billy reaches into his pocket and he takes out a gun and he lays it on the bar. And he says, "I was going to shoot you when you come in, but she talked me out of it." See, now the logic of this escapes me. "You gonna shoot me, for what? Shoot her. I ain't done nothing to you, don't even know you." Shoot her.

See, and all of a sudden the idea of dying young got real serious. See, because I don't want to die. I'm twenty years old, just starting out life. I don't want my mother to have to come to my funeral. See, because I'm supposed to go to her funeral. And those of you whose mothers are still alive, I do not envy you. There will come a day when you will suffer the most profound grief imaginable. And you look up and you find out that all them years you been living on your mother's prayers and now you've got to live on your own.

See, but right now, I'm in the 88 Bar and the gun's on the counter and I'm thinking what to do. I'm thinking that maybe I should try and grab for the gun. But see, if I grab for the gun then he's gonna get mad and if I'm successful then I'm going to end up shooting him. And then, I'm going to jail. Forever. And if I grab for the gun and ain't successful then he going to be mad and he gonna shoot me. And then I'm gonna be dead. Forever. And right about then, the bartender comes down and say, "Hey, buddy you gotta put that in your pocket. You can't leave that here on the bar. You gotta put that in your pocket." And then, the bartender walks away! I wanted to say, "Hey, no man, come back." Then, Billy says, "Can I buy you a beer?" And I wanted to say, "No, man, I'm trying to get the hell away from you." But I go, "Yeah, man, you can buy me a beer." No, now that's not the way I said it. I go, *(Deep voice.)* "Yeah, man, you can buy me a beer."

He buying me this beer and then he starts telling me how much he love Snookie and how she told him she love me and all this stuff. And I ain't really listening to him. And then, he started crying. See, and I thought I was scared before. 'Cause this the last thing I want to see. See, this is the last thing you want to see. A distraught nigger with a gun. And you sleeping with his wife. So, he cries and all that and then he gets up. And he leaves the bar. He tells me, "Man, take good care of her." Then he leaves the bar.

She starts talking to me. But really my mind is racing. I'm thinking. Trying to figure out what I'm going to do. What am I going to do? And she's trying to say something to me, but I'm not listening to her. I ain't even looking at her. Because I'm thinking, "What should I do? If I leave now, maybe he's waiting outside the bar to shoot me, for when I get out there. But, then maybe he's gone up the street and if he's gone up the street, I don't want to give him time to change his mind and like, come back. All I know is like, he's not in the bar now." So I'm saying, "Well, man, if he's out there going to shoot you when you come out, then you just dead. But you be a damn fool if you stay here and give him an opportunity to change his mind and come back and shoot you." So, I decide, I was going to leave. And I got up and she's like, "August…" And I started walking to the door. And I tell myself, "Now, you do understand you could be dead in ten seconds. You do understand that?" And I go, "Yeah, I understand that." "Alright then, keep going, goddammit, don't you dare stop. Don't stop. Keep going." And I forced myself to walk out. And, I get outside the door and like, ain't nobody, nowhere. And I started running this way. See, I wanted to go this way. But, I ain't thinking. And I ran as far as I could, for as long as I could, until I got tired. I got tired and I say, "Okay, man, it's alright. You still alive man. She set you up. She set you up, man."

And that's when I learned to cut my losses early. So I called Snookie, "Baby, listen... I'm coming to get my things." Now, I saw Snookie the last time I was in Pittsburgh. She's still a very beautiful woman. She's married to Reginald Howze. They been married for twenty-seven years and she got three kids. She's beautiful, but she just wasn't the woman for me, at that time. Thank God.

See, because, this woman done set me on the road to hell with that reefer. This woman almost got me killed in the Oyster House. This woman almost got me killed in the 88 Bar. And I ain't known her, but three months. I figure if I hung out with her too much longer, I really would end up in an early grave. So, I go where? Back up to my mother's house.

(Typing...)

CHAWLEY WILLIAMS

Chawley Williams was a poet, man. And Chawley was also a junkie. Chawley would sit in a corner and as he put it "lick the face of God." He was a heroin addict. See, but, I didn't pass judgment on people, still don't. You know? Like Chawley, was Chawley. Chawley was my friend.

So, like, one day, we're sitting down at my house, me, him and another guy and they were shooting up dope. And the guy had the needle stuck in his arm and he looks at me and he says, "Hey, August man, you want some of this?" And before I could say anything. Chawley had grabbed him and slammed his head into the wall. Chawley said, "That's August, man, that's August. Don't you never offer him none of that shit. Don't you never offer him none of that shit. Man, that's August, man." And I said, "Chawley, man, I wasn't gonna take, man." See, but Chawley saw something in me. And Chawley didn't want me to become a heroin addict like him. You see and I realize that all of these years, I have worked to reward that thing that Chawley see in me.

So, one day, Chawley said to me, he said, "Come on man, I want to introduce you to a friend of mine. I'm gonna take you up and introduce you to Cy Morocco."

(Typing…)

CY MOROCCO

So, we went up to Cy's house. And when I met Cy, Cy was sitting at this desk. And he had this big, thick book on astronomy. And Cy was sitting there reading this book. And Cy had a skylight in his apartment and I looked around and I didn't see a telescope. So, I figure that's in the pawnshop, you know. But Cy is like this real, heavy dude.

So, Chawley's like, "Well, me and August, we going across the street to this little restaurant. Why don't you come over." And Cy said, "Okay." And he come over and Cy was wearing a sport coat. And I said, "Say, hey man, I like that coat." And Cy said, "Here, man, you want it?" And he start taking off his coat. And I go, "Nah, man, I don't want it. I just…" And Cy said, "That's alright, you can have it. I go get another one." So, he gave me his coat. Then he went back across the street to get another one. And I looked at Chawley, man, and Chawley say, "Yeah, man. That's just the way Cy is." And I say, "Well, I'm glad I didn't say I like his pants."

But that was Cy Morocco.

I had a friend, Gerry Rhodes, who wrote a story about Cy, which he called "The Ugliest Man in the World." See, and Gerry Rhodes was being generous. You know? 'Cause, it's a fact. Cy was one ugly dude. But he was a very beautiful person, you understand.

The next time I saw Cy, Cy had a saxophone strap hanging around his neck. And he was going around putting up these flyers on telephone booths. And they said, "Cy Morocco. Aurora Club. 11:30 p.m." So, Cy say, "Hey, August man, you going to come down and hear me play?" I say, "Yeah, man. I didn't know you play saxophone. Yeah, down at Aurora Club around 11:30? Yeah, I ain't doing nothing, I'll be down there."

So, I went down to the Aurora Club. And I found out that 11:30 is the time in which they let anybody sit in with the band. But see, Cy done went out and put up his own posters and Cy got his fan club here, of which I am a member. So, Cy's turn come and Cy get up on the bandstand and he say, "Night in Tunisia." And the band starting playing and Cy started playing. And then the band stopped. See, 'cause Cy can't play saxophone. He just up there making a lot of noise.

And I saw that. Another lesson I learned in life. Say, "August, you want to be a writer, right? Learn how to do it. Don't be like Cy. Don't try to push your spirit out through a horn that you don't know how to play. Learn how to play the saxophone."

See… Cy Morocco was John Coltrane. In spirit. Cy just didn't know how to play the saxophone.

(Typing…)

COLTRANE

Now in 1966, John Coltrane was widely considered the most creative and innovative figure on the jazz saxophone. His contributions to the musical art form, jazz, are without peer and unparalleled. But it didn't mean nothing to me. Because, jazz didn't mean anything to me, because it didn't have any words. And I was a poet, and music without words didn't mean nothing to me. But all that changed on an October night in 1966 when I walked up and saw a hundred people standing on a corner. It ain't nothing, as I said earlier, to see a hundred people standing on a corner. Two hundred people standing on a corner. But they usually be down at Center and Kirkpatrick. They were up at Wylie and Kirkpatrick. And when I saw them, I said to myself, "Oh, something must've happened." I figured somebody got killed. And I ran up and I said, "Hey, what's happening?" Everybody went, "Shh."

(Muffled up-tempo saxophone plays.*)

---

*Licensees should use a song in the public domain or create an original composition.

Crawford Grill. And they were listening to John Coltrane. They were listening to the music. It filtered out. You see, to go inside the Crawford Grill you had to pay a cover charge and the drinks cost ninety cents. See, down the street they thirty-five cents. But these people, they can't afford to go inside to hear John Coltrane. But the music is coming out over the heads of the patrons of the bar...

(The sound of the up-tempo saxophone comes out over the heads of the patrons inside.)

John Coltrane ain't playing for the patrons of the bar, he playing for them guys outside. Because the people inside the bar, they don't even know how to pronounce John Coltrane's name. They sitting there talking about what they gonna do next weekend. "Did you hear so-and-so got a new Buick." See, John Coltrane is background music to them. But for the guys outside they see it as their weapon. Music is their shield. And in order to understand that you'd have to understand that this...

(A prayer on saxophone plays.)

...This music is the thing that has enabled them to survive the most outrageous insults. Brought to America in chains. Defined as property. Bought and sold and traded like so many shares of IBM. Suffered hundreds of years of degradation and indignity on top of indignity. Made to drink from a fountain of bitterness in a Christian country that espouses freedom and justice as the pillars of its society. They have prepared the harvest and watched the taskmasters carry the barrels away to the cellar. "But that's okay, I got this."

(Up-tempo saxophone resumes.)

It remains one of the most remarkable moments of my life. To see two hundred niggers stunned into silence by the power of art and the soaring music of John Coltrane and his exploration of man's connection to the divinity. And the power of possibility of human life.

(Up-tempo saxophone overwhelms the house!)

I had a friend of mine who met John Coltrane. A man named Carl Jennings. And Carl told me this story. He said, a friend of his introduced him to John. He said "John, I want you to meet a friend of mine, Carl Jennings. Carl plays saxophone." And John Coltrane looked at him and said, "You play saxophone?" And Carl said, "Yeah." And John Coltrane said, "Teach me something." And he looked at him. [And John Coltrane] said, "Yeah, you know, what you're working on." And Carl said, "I'm working on my scales." He said, "Oh, that's good. That's good. Keep working on your scales." And then John Coltrane turned away and went to find somebody who could teach him something. You see, because when you on a search, just possibly you can't afford to leave any stone unturned. Most of them gonna turn up snails. But you still got to overturn them. And just possibly, Carl Jennings, beginning saxophone player, had something that John Coltrane, master saxophone player, great, creative innovator had missed, and that he needed to know in order for him to complete his search. John Coltrane died an untimely death in 1967, at the age of thirty-nine and he never found what he was looking for. But see, I know a man who did...

We were performing plays at A. Leo Weill Elementary School auditorium. And, one day a man walked in. He was a small, slightly built shy man. And he said, "Can I uh, play the piano?" There was a piano in the auditorium. And we looked at him and we said, "Can you play? Yeah, man, go ahead. We can't play. If you can play, yeah, go ahead and play."

And then this man sat down and began to make this most incredible music come out of this piano. We talking about world-class piano. We talking about Art Tatum. He begin to play that piano...

(Art Tatum's "Tiger Rag" begins to play.)

"Look at that little, motherfucker play, man. Hot damn, man." And he's playing this piano and all of sudden he stopped –

(Music stops.)

He stopped and he banged his head on the piano. He busted his head open. He begin to hit the piano and he kick it and all the while he's screaming, "[Repeatedly unintelligible phrase.]" And we grabbed him and we wrestled him down. "[Repeatedly unintelligible phrase.] Limitay...Limitation of...Limitation of the instrument. Limitation of the instrument."

(Typing...)

LIMITATION OF THE INSTRUMENT

Limitation of the instrument. See, that's where John Coltrane was trying to go. That's what every artist is trying to get to. The limitation of the instrument. And see, when this first happened, I misunderstood it. I thought he heard something that he couldn't play. But he didn't say he was limited. He said the instrument was limited.

See, in order to understand that, all you gotta do was imagine Pablo Picasso standing in front of a blank canvas with a paintbrush in his hand and suddenly go, "Limitation of the instrument. There ain't nothing else I can do with this paint and canvas. I done did it all. This is limiting me. I got to find another way to express myself."

See, I think that's where every artist wants to go. That's where I want to go. I'm going to write 'til I'm ninety-seven. But, if you ever hear somebody say, "Did you hear about August, man. He quit." You go, "Oh yeah. He must've found the limitation of the instrument. But, I did hear he's playing saxophone now."

(Typing...)

CY MOROCCO

Cy Morocco... Cy would come up to you and Cy would have a *Time* magazine and he would hand it to you. He'd say, "Read this and see if you got what I got." And then I'd read it and Cy would say, "What'd you get?" I'd say, "I got such and such, and such and such." Cy would say, "Yeah, that's the same thing I got." And then Cy would go and walk up to Rob and say, "Hey Rob. Say, man, I was reading this and it say such and such, and such and such." And Cy would do this all the time.

And so, Cy asked to see some of my poems. And I told Chawley that "Cy wants to see some of my poems." And Chawley looked at me and said, "Man, Cy can't read." I said, "You bullshitting man. He was reading a book when I met him." He go, "Naw, man. He was looking at them pictures and them planets and things. Cy can't read." I said, "Aw, man. You lying." He said, "No. Don't he come up and ask you to read something and see if you got the same thing that he got?" I go, "Yeah." He said, "See. He can't read, but he want to know the information. Cy don't want nobody to know he can't read." I said, "I'll be damned, man." 'Cause Cy was a smart man. You know he found a way to get the information. He was also a very dignified man. So, he didn't want people to know he couldn't read. But, he found out a way to get the information without you knowing that.

And as the time went on, Cy lost his mind. And Cy knew he lost it, because he went around looking for it. And he would come up to you and he would ask you, "Have you seen it?" And, I go, "No, Cy. Man, I ain't seen it Cy." He go, "Yeah, August, man. I've got to find my mind. I'm still looking for it, man. You ain't seen it?" I said, "Nah, Cy." "Got to find my mind, August. Got to find it." And then he'd wander off.

Cy would come up to you and he'd say, "August, see I got something for you." And he'd reach in his pocket and he'd pull out this rock and he would present it to you like it was the Hope Diamond. And he'd say, "A piece of this earth." And, I'd take the rock and say, "Thanks, Cy."

I still got some of them rocks Cy gave me. See I have two daughters and when one of them was a little girl, she'd come up to me and say, "Daddy, you want this rock?" And that reminds me of Cy. 'Cause I think they both know something that we don't.

The only time I know the police to ever do anything halfway decent was they would occasionally grab Cy Morocco and take him down to the jail and force him to take a shower and give him some clothes that they had brought from home and like turn him loose.

And Cy was – I called Cy, he was the original homeless man. And I would look at Cy sometimes and I often thought – See, Cy was an African. But, he was an African lost in America. 'Cause when you're African in America there's adjustments and things that you have to make. 'Cause, your natural impulse is different than the way things are done. But Cy had trouble making that adjustment.

(*Typing...*)

AFRICAN IN AMERICA

You see because, we a people who crowd the popcorn counter. See, white people form a line. There be like two white people and a third white person will come up and stand behind them. And then, four and five. And there'd be an empty space at the counter. So, a black person will go to the empty space. And they go to the empty space and someone'll go, "Excuse me, but there's a line back here." And like, sure enough there is a line. It's not like, you don't know how to go stand in line. But, it's like it's just against everything, because you a different people.

See, white people will look at them big screen TV's and they go, "Hey, man, how many inches do you think that is?" See, and black folks will look at them same TV's and go, "Joe, how much you think that weigh?"

One time I was in the bus station in St. Paul, and I saw these six Japanese Americans having breakfast. They sat there, chatted politely among themselves, one of them actually got up and took pictures. Now I found out from their conversation that they were taking the Greyhound across the country to go to college. They can all afford to fly first class but they taking a bus, they having an adventure, having fun. So when the bill came, they all reached for their American Express cards to pay, then paid the bill and left.

So I asked myself, if it had been six black guys in here having breakfast, what would be the difference? First thing I noticed is that none of the Japanese guys played the jukebox. But six black guys walk in, the first thing they do, somebody gonna go over to the jukebox and put in a quarter, right? Then another guy gonna come and say, "Hey, Rodney man, play so-and-so!" "Naw, man, play your own record. Put your own quarter in there."

The second thing I noticed, nobody said nothing to the waitress. Now six black guys, I don't care what she look like, somebody gonna say something to her. "Hey baby, how you doing?" "Look here, mama, what's your phone number?" "Naw, naw, don't talk to him, he can't read. Give *me* your phone number."

And then the guy gonna get up to play another song, somebody gonna steal a piece of bacon off his plate, and he's gonna come back and say,

"Hey man, I ain't playing with you all, man, quit messing with my food." When the time comes to pay the bill, it's going to be, "Hey Leroy, lend me two dollars, man." Right? It's just the way we do it.

Now if you were a white person observing that, you would say, "They're loud, they don't like each other. The guy wouldn't let him play the record, the guy stole food off his plate, they harassed the waitress." So to that white person observing, the way we do things is all wrong. If you bring six white guys in, they'll do it differently than the Japanese and the black guys. But what white America does, it accepts the way the Japanese does it.

It accepts the way the Czechs from the Czech Republic might do things different. But blacks are supposed to act like them. White America says, "You all still ain't learned how to do things."

Just like I had a friend of mine. He went down to get a job as a disc jockey at a radio station. It was a hard rock station, but he know the music. He know it better than anybody I know. But, he didn't get hired. So, I said, "You know why they didn't hire you, don't you?" He say, "Why?" I say, "Because, you outrageously wicked. You a violator of public regulations. Sullen. Hostile. Menacing. And affected by an undesirable condition." And he looked at me and he said in his best radio disc jockey voice, "Yeah, you right abou, aah baah, aah baah, aah bout that."

(Typing…)

WRONG THING, WRONG TIME

You can say the wrong thing, to the wrong person at the right time and get away with it. But you cannot say the wrong thing, to the wrong person at the wrong time.

So, being a young man, I was out looking for female companionship. And, I went into this bar and I didn't see anybody in the bar and I was on my way out of the bar and the man who was in front of me was on his way out of the bar and there was a man coming into the bar. And the man coming into the bar had a white woman with him. And the man coming out of the bar said, "Say, Philmore. See, you got your white ho with you."

Those were the last words that that man spoke in his life. "Say, Philmore. See, you got your white ho with you." See, 'cause, Philmore pulled out his knife. And Philmore said, "That's my wife, motherfucker, that's my wife, motherfucker." And he hit the man with the knife. And the man put his arm up and he cut his arm. And then he cut the man on his face. And then he cut the man's throat. And the man fell down on the ground, but Philmore didn't stop. "That's my wife, motherfucker. That's my wife." Somebody tried to pull him off. "Get the fuck off me. That's my wife, motherfucker. That's my wife, motherfucker." And he continued to hit this man over and over and over again. And blood was flying everywhere, until he got tired. His arm got tired and he couldn't move it anymore. And he folded up his knife and he put it in his pocket and he went and got in his car and drove off.

And the police come. Ain't nobody saw nothing. "Nah, he just started bleeding." That's a phenomenon that I'm trying to figure out too. Right?

So, what's happening here? The man didn't mean any harm. "Hey, Philmore." He trying to say, "Hi." See, but he said the wrong thing, to the wrong person, at the wrong time.

But what Philmore's doing is the same thing that them Prussian officers in them Guy de Maupassant stories are doing, when they challenging them guys to duels. He defending the honor of his wife. He just – it's his way of doing it.

Which is why, when the police come, nobody see nothing. Why? He deserve to die. You don't insult nobody's wife like that. See, the community understands this. They're facing a sanction. Either sanction conduct, or they don't. But this man was wrong. Now, if Philmore cut the man because he trying to rob the man. Somebody say, "Yeah, Philmore did it. See, he went in that car over there."

(*Typing…*)

SHUT MOUTH

So one day, I was hanging out with Chawley. We were on Center Avenue and this guy comes up and he says, "Say man, you seen Dokes." And I say, "Yeah, he standing right there. Right in front of the Ellis Hotel." And the guy walked off.

And Chawley said to me, "What he want to see Dokes about?" I said, "I don't know." "What if he go up there and kill him? Then you done put the finger on him. You done told him where he at. Say, man, you don't know where nobody's at. You don't know where nobody live at. You don't know nothing, man. Let him find out on his own." I go, "Yeah. Okay, I got that." "It makes sense to me. It's logical. Okay, yeah. I got that."

Wasn't but two weeks later, I'm standing on Center Avenue and a white guy comes up on a motorcycle. Come to find out he's an actor. Not only was he an actor, he was in Michael McClure's play called *The Beard* about Billy the Kid and Jean Harlow in Hell. And here's the guy that played Billy the Kid. And I was impressed with that because it was sort of like he knew Jean Harlow. You know? So, I got to talking with him and I introduce him to Chawley. See, actor and poet. And him and Chawley, man they got along. And him and Chawley walked off together. Man, that's cool. They like each other. I did that. I introduced them. I found Chawley a friend. About 10:30 that night, the actor, I forget his name, but let's call him Joe. Joe comes up on his motorcycle and he says, "Hey, August, you know where Chawley live at?" And I go, "Yeah, man."

Now what did Chawley just tell me, two weeks before? See, I didn't learn nothing have I?

"Oh, yeah, man." He said, "Show me." "Yeah." So, I hop on the motorcycle. Now, you have to understand. Chawley lives in the projects. You can get lost in the projects and spend six months trying to find your way out. Sometimes, Chawley can't find his way home. And here, I take him through this labyrinth, this maze, that Jorge Borges would be proud of. And I take him right to Chawley's door. And I knock on the door. And Jeanine says, "Who is it?"

Now, Jeanine was Chawley's wife. She was a very beautiful woman. And Jeanine could cook. Jeanine could cook better than my mother. And you had to go a ways there. I ate many, many a dinner up at Jeanine's house, 'cause I was always hanging out with Chawley.

So Jeanine says, "Who is it?" I say, "August and Joe." She say, "Chawley ain't here." And I turned to Joe and I say, "Well, Chawley ain't home, man." And Joe kicked the door. And Joe began hollering and cussing and threatening to kill Chawley. And threatening to kill Chawley's wife. And threatening to kill Chawley's kids.

See, because when I made that introduction of actor – poet. It was really an introduction of junkie – to – junkie. And the guy was looking for some drugs when he come up to me. But when he come up to me, he come up to the wrong person. And he quickly found that out, without ever mentioning the word "drugs." And then I turned him onto the right person. And then they go off and Chawley beat him for some money, which he would've got away with if it hadn't been for me. And I went and brought him right to Chawley. "Goddammit, man. I fucked up big time." Joe was enraged. He jumped on his motorcycle and drives off into the night. And I said, "Man, I've got to face Chawley."

So, the next day, I'm standing down on Center Avenue and Chawley come up to me and Chawley said... *(Silent but animated cussing out.)* Then he walked off. And then I said,

"Phew." See, I was disappointed though, because I had let Chawley down, you know? But, I'm learning.

So, that afternoon I'm in the Halfway Art Gallery and I see Jeanine. And Jeanine comes in and I say, "Hi, Jeanine." And Jeanine reaches in her purse and pulls out a hunting knife. Like one of them Bowie knives. And she's coming at me with the knife. And I'm laughing because, you know, this is Jeanine, and this is August. "Man, that's Jeanine, man." And she kept coming. And I'm like, "Hey, Jeanine." And I picked up this chair. You know because she kept coming at me. But me, I'm still laughing. This is still like funny because it's Jeanine. And she's got the knife and coming after me, August. She kept coming and I put out the chair and then she swung the knife. And when she swung the knife, she hit the chair. And when she hit the chair a piece of wood went flying from the chair. And that's when I got real serious about staying alive. See, because, she wasn't trying to hit the chair, she was trying to hit me. And now I've got the chair, and I'm trying to keep her off and I'm trying to think what to do. Because, we don't know how this is going to turn out. And I'm thinking that maybe I should bust her on the head with the chair, but then I have to leave myself exposed and nobody ever told me what to do if somebody pulls a knife on you. So, I didn't know the art of exactly how to go about, all I know is I can't let her cut me. And right in the middle of all that a guy grabbed her. Thank God. And wrestled her out of the gallery. I have not seen, or heard of Jeanine since then. And that's however many years ago.

I can't count. The reason why my math is so bad is because of Sister Mary Eldephonse. She was my seventh-grade math teacher. She didn't like me and I didn't like her. And I thought, "If you teaching it, I ain't learning it." Now I say I can't count. See, if you say, "August, how many years is it from 1966 to 1984?" I go, "Let's see sixty-six, seventy-six and eighty-four. Right?" But, if you owed me eighty-four dollars and walked up and handed me sixty-six. I'd say, "Man, where my eighteen dollars?" So, some things you know how to count.

(Typing...)

ORAL SEX

Let's skip that one.

(Typing...)

NANCY IRELAND

Nancy Ireland... Nancy Ireland was a girl in the seventh grade that even the third-graders were in love with. I used to write poems for Nancy Ireland and I would like leave them on her desk. Nancy would like read the poem and then she would like smile and look and look at Anthony Kirvin. See, 'cause I didn't put my name on the poem. I was too shy to do that. But I was in love with Nancy Ireland, as was everyone. And when Sister Mary Eldephonse announced that the seventh grade were putting on a Christmas pageant and everybody knew that Nancy Ireland was going to play the Virgin Mary. And I wanted to play the role of Joseph, so I could play opposite her. And then the day came when Sister Mary Eldephonse announced the casting. "The role of the Virgin Mary will be played by (surprise) Nancy Ireland. The Three Wise Men will be played by Claude Fountain, Eddie Chambers and Reginald Howze. And the role of Joseph will be played by Anthony Kirvin." See, Anthony Kirvin stuttered. And me and Catherine Moran were the best readers in the class. And yet, Anthony Kirvin got the lead role in the play. And, "Catherine Moran will play the narrator. Robert Jenkins will play the Innkeeper. And Freddie Kittel (which was myself, my name in those days) will play the cymbals." As in brass, concave instruments that sounded when striking together. A non-speaking role! I was outraged.

We had rehearsal after school. We didn't have any cymbals. We had to borrow them from another school and we had to wait until their Christmas pageant was over until we got the cymbals. So I had to rehearse by clapping my hands together. Catherine Moran would give me the cue and "Lo, the Three Wise Men arrived at the manger of the Christ child" and then I would clang the cymbals together. Well, Anthony's stuttering added an hour to rehearsal. Our laughter added another hour, but you see what a glorious week it was. You see because you won't know this, but everybody else, the Virgin Mary, Joseph, the Three Wise Men, and the Innkeeper are all inside the drama. They over here. And there are two people who are outside the drama. That's the Narrator, Catherine Moran and the cymbal player. And it was during that week that I discovered Catherine Moran. And you see, that although I had went to school with Catherine Moran since the third grade, I never really looked at her. So now, in retrospect, I discover that she was always there, wherever I was, looking at me. And she was a small, waif-like girl with jet-black hair, deep black eyes, which now terrified me every time I looked into them. She became the sum total of my world and occupied my every thought. I felt somehow that this was unearned. That in order to earn it I would have to do something. So, I vowed that before the pageant was over I was going to kiss her. Only, I didn't know how, I didn't know where. The day of the pageant arrives. We arrived early. Sister Mary Eldephonse is rushing about making last minute preparations. We were supposed to dress in the bathroom and then make our entrance after the adults had come and were seated. And "Oh, by the way, the cymbals have arrived and they're upstairs in the cloakroom go and get them." So, I get up to the cloakroom and there's Catherine Moran rummaging about in the cloakroom. And Catherine says, "I come to get you your cymbals." My cymbals. See, all of a sudden, playing the cymbals is the most important role in the play. And she picked up the cymbals and she handed them to me. And that was like handing Sir Lancelot his sword. You see in the fire of that gesture, our star burning in its zenith, in the heat of the moment, in the cloister of the cloakroom I kissed her. Brief. Electric. The kiss was witness and sanction and it deepened our conspiracy. And I knew that years later I would have to travel through the province of unsettled schoolboys searching for the fleshy comforts of conquest. The wild, exclamatory music of sorority girls in full surrender and secret knowing of riotous muscle. But here, now, that kiss held us in the conspiracy of boundless joy. So, we go downstairs. The adults have taken their place. The pageant began. Anthony Kirvin braces up under the moment and he doesn't stutter. And then I hear, "Lo, the Three Wise Men arrive at the manger of the Christ child." And I turned and I looked at Catherine Moran and she had this light coming out of her. It was a luminosity that was burnished with the remarkable instance of our secret kiss and no one or no thing had ever been more beautiful. I did not clang the cymbals at my cue. It was somewhere later when the Three Wise Men were presenting their gifts that it occurred to me that I hadn't done it and I thought maybe may as well do it now. You see, the sudden clash of cymbals was a celebration of the brief syllabus of our desire and there was a roaring conclusion to its own gospel. Because whatever angels that thrashed above our heads I was calling them to witness so that no testimony be mute. It was many years before I was to see the light of that grace again. I would travel many roads and cross many deserts until I came to Sumaria, and sat by the well, and a woman came walking out of the desert, molded by light, and shaped by the thought and the presence of something infinitely larger than the moment that had been so long in coming. And having such beauty that the sheer weight of her billowing dress, its hot tempers pressed in on me and I grabbed and held onto morning's light and that's when I met my wife, Constanza Romero. I asked for water and she gave me wine.

I have never seen, nor heard from, or about Catherine Moran, since I changed schools the following year. But, wherever she is I hope that God continues to shine the light of his grace down upon her. Bless her with sweet water, temperate climate and many, many grandchildren.

(Typing...)

PAT'S PLACE

When I lived in Pittsburgh I used to go a place called Pat's Place. And that's where these old men of the community would congregate, the elders of the community. And I would stand around and I would listen to them, trying to learn something about life. And then in 1978, I moved to Saint Paul.

And in 1979, I was visiting Pittsburgh and one of the old men called me over to him. He called me, Youngblood. He say, "Youngblood." I go, "Yes, sir." He said, "I heard you moved." And I said, "Yes sir, I moved to Minnesota." He said, "Well how often do you get back to Pittsburgh?" And I said, "Well, I get back about twice a year." And he said, "Well, I ain't going to be here when you come back. But, I want to tell you this. I've been watching you for about six or seven years now. See, and you going through life carrying a ten-gallon bucket. And if you go through life carrying a ten-gallon bucket, you always going to be disappointed. 'Cause it ain't never going to be filled." And he said, "Don't you go through life carrying no ten-gallon bucket. Get you a little cup and carry that through life. And that way somebody put a little bit in it and then you have something." And I go, "Yes, sir."

I do want you to know that since then I have been working on it and I have got it cut down to about a gallon bucket. But, I do want you to know this also. That it ain't never going to get down to that little cup. See, and it ain't never going to get down to that little cup because I deserve more.

(*Typing...*)

WILLING TO DIE

I was in Los Angeles one time and I got a check from the Mark Taper Forum for seven hundred and fifty dollars. And I took that check down to the bank. The same bank on which it was drawn. In which the Mark Taper Forum banks about thirteen million dollars a year. And I presented the check, along with my identification card to the woman behind the counter. And she picked up my identification card and she said, "Where'd you get this?" And I said, "It's a Washington State ID" (*The woman said.*) "Is this your name on here?" (*I said.*) "Of course, it's my name." (*She said.*) "Just a minute." Then she turned and walked off and went into this room. You see, now, when I go to the bank I try not to get behind a Black person in the line. See, because I know that the line's going to get held up because they're going to triple-check everything. Alright? So, after about five minutes she comes out with a man. And the man doesn't come over to where I'm standing but he looks at me. And then they go over to this book and they're turning the pages in the book. And I notice as they're turning the pages that the book is a book that contains photographs of all the official State ID's. It took them awhile, but they found Washington. And they're looking at it and it's like "Yes, everything's in the right place. Yes it's the ID. Yes, it looks like it. We're gonna have to give this nigger this seven hundred and fifty dollars." So, the woman came and she counted out the seven hundred and fifty dollars. Then she stood there. And I said, "Can I have an envelope please?" And she said, "We don't have envelopes at this bank." And I asked myself, I said, "August, are you willing to die over this?" And I said, "Nah, this ain't nothing worth dying over." And I picked up my seven hundred and fifty dollars, put it in my pocket and I left.

See, but I do want you to know that I went back to that bank two weeks later and I got a different teller and I got my check cashed without incident and I said to her, "Can I have an envelope please?" And she reached under the counter and she handed me an envelope. And I said, "Well, the other teller told me that you didn't have envelopes at this bank." And she said, "I don't know what she told you." Which was true, she didn't know. But I knew. And God knew. See, 'cause she going to Hell.

See, she thinks that's a little thing. But it's not a little thing. She looked at a man and she said, "This man does not deserve the same respect as other men deserve." And that's the sin that caused slavery. You see, so when she die and she go before God, God's going to say to her, he gonna say, "You pushed your sister down the steps when you were nine years old. You ran over that dog in the parking lot. You embezzled money from the church. You fucked your brother-in-law. He said, "But I forgive, I understand all that. But you lied to that man about not having an envelope and ain't thought nothing about what me, God, was gonna think about it. You were willing to put a mark on your soul over a goddamn envelope, so you go to Hell." Which, was the same thing I told her.

Now I would like to tell you that when we came to this part in rehearsal, I would stop and talk about this envelope for like an hour. And someone said, "August, man, what is it about the envelope? That's a little thing." And I go, "No, it's not a little thing." You see 'cause it's not about an envelope. I don't care anything about an envelope. I got lots of envelopes. It's about R-E-S-P-E-C-T. See when I taught my course at Dartmouth I told my students, "Demand respect from everyone. The government, your schools, your church, your parents, your lover, yourself. Demand respect. If it cost you your life then you have lived a good life and died an honorable death. Demand respect. It's not about an envelope. It's about P-R-I-N-C-I-P-L-E-S. Principles by which I have lived my entire life.

(Typing...)

HOW DO YOU KNOW, WHAT YOU KNOW

How do you know, what you know? You don't.

How do you know you know it? How do I know that I learned to keep my mouth shut? Even though when I saw that guy get killed, I didn't speak to nobody for the next six months. 'Cause I was afraid I was going to say the wrong thing. But have I learned that? We don't know. It is yet to be determined. See, I could go out there right now, tonight and say the wrong thing, to the wrong person at the wrong time. And then you all would be saying, "You hear what happened to August? He should've kept his damn mouth shut."

So, you don't know that you know anything. Until you know, you know it. And that's the most important lesson that I've learned, is to take all your truths, all your empirical truths that you have learned in your life and do not try to place them in a hierarchy and decide which one is more important than the other. Because you don't know.

In order to do that you would have to measure one against the other. And any time you start measuring, what's going to happen? You measure wrong.

> *(During the following the* **ACTOR** *crosses to coat rack, gets the other sport coat and the Borsalino that has been hanging there since preshow – sets out the Borsalino on the dictionary, puts on the sport coat.)*

To arrive at this moment in my life, I have traveled many roads, some circuitous, some brambled and rough, some sharp and straight, and all of them have led as if by some grand design to the one burnished with art and small irrevocable tragedies. I've carried in my pocket, to bargain my passage, memory and a wild heart that plies its trade with considerate and sometimes alarming passion. I have the temper of a rascal which has served me more often than not in good stead. Though there have been occasions in which it has been problematic.

My mouth – which has known both prayer and curses – does not bite itself and has often called to its courage and had it answer. On the occasions it has faltered I have learned to speak eloquently on the virtues of silence and its golden halo.

Some roads have opened to me. Other roads have bred landscapes of severe wolves to blunt and discourage my advance. Still, others, closed for repair, shall remain closed and wanting forever.

Yet, I do not stand here and say that we African Americans are victims, but rather we both, black and white are victims of our history and our victimization leaves us staring at each other across a great divide of economics, privilege, and the unmitigated pursuit of happiness.

We are not Black by the accident of our births. Our births are moments of profound creativity engineered by our genetic muscle as it aspires toward perfection.

(A musical Spiritual Baptism of atavistic signature and ritual begins to play* as the **ACTOR** *reveals the poem in his pocket...)*

We are what we are –
Are made by old things,
Come back. Clearly,
Brilliant as the sun.

(As the **ACTOR** *gives the poem to an audience member, the music grows...)*

(During the following sequence of typing...the **ACTOR** *turns his back to the audience, puts on the Borsalino, conjuring the silhouette of August Wilson watching the titles of his works of art...)*

MA RAINEY'S BLACK BOTTOM

FENCES

JOE TURNER'S COME AND GONE

THE PIANO LESSON

TWO TRAINS RUNNING

SEVEN GUITARS

JITNEY

KING HEDLEY II

GEM OF THE OCEAN

RADIO GOLF

(The silhouette of August Wilson vanishes into the crucible as:)

(Final typing...)

AUGUST WILSON

---

*Licensees should use a song in the public domain or create an original composition.

9780573705892